The Ghost I Am

Mariz Everly

To my husband and my precious kids,

I'm always here

PREFACE

Stories about life and death have always fascinated me—not just the endings, but the in-between spaces where emotions linger, where questions remain unanswered. I wanted to explore what it means to hold on to something so tightly that it keeps you from moving forward, even when everything around you changes.

Ellie's story is about a girl who couldn't leave her home, trapped not by walls but by her own unanswered questions. As I began to write, she became more than just a character; she became a reflection of all the things we struggle to let go of: pain, regret, and the fear of facing the truth.

But this isn't just a story about grief or loss—it's a story about connection. Ellie's bond with her family, her mysterious little companion, and even herself drives this book forward. It's about finding the courage to confront what's holding you back and learning to let go, even when it feels impossible.

I created the concept of The Ghost I Am because I think, in some way, we've all been Ellie at some point in our lives. Maybe not trapped in a literal sense, but stuck in a place we can't seem to escape, haunted by questions we're too afraid to answer.

This story is for anyone who's felt that way. It's for anyone who's ever wondered what it would take to find peace.

PROLOGUE

When you die, they don't tell you what comes next.

I thought maybe I'd see a bright light, feel the warmth of some great, unknowable love. Or maybe it'd be nothing—a quiet, endless nothing where I wouldn't have to think or feel ever again.

But what I got was this.

This house. These walls. The same rooms I lived in, laughed in, cried in. Only now, I'm just… here. Watching. Listening. Feeling. And no one knows I'm still around.

I don't know why I can't leave. Maybe I've forgotten something. Or maybe something's holding me back. I try not to think about it too much because when I do, it feels like drowning.

But here's the worst part: I don't remember how I died.

I can't put it together. It's like the truth is sitting just out of reach, taunting me, waiting for me to be ready.

And then there's her.

I thought I was alone, but one night, I found her—a little girl with wide, curious eyes and a silence that says more than words ever could. She doesn't speak, but she sees me.

And somehow, I think she's part of the answer.

This isn't the afterlife I expected. But it's mine. And if I'm going to figure out why I'm still here, I have to face everything I tried so hard to forget.

CHAPTER 1—

DEAD AND COLD

The house is too quiet, except for the sound of the fridge humming. I watched them, alive but they looked dead inside. Mom, Dad, and Ned. I'm here but I am not. I thought when you die, you can have—peace, clarity, and maybe even a big bright light that takes you to where you're supposed to go. But no. I'm stuck here. I am still here.

Im dead.

The truth is that it's colder than I have ever imagined. Just like this house. This house feels hollow and empty. I looked in the mirror. I see myself looking faint. My hair hangs lifeless. My eyes are unsettling. They look hollow, still searching for the piece that I lost. I do not remember what happened to me.

How did I die?

I know this house—we lived here since the day I was born. I know Mom's quiet strength, Dad's crazy dad jokes, and Ned's endless curiosity about the moon and the stars. But now, there is a space between me and my family. I can hear them, I can see them, but I can't touch them. I am in the house but feel far away in the darkest part of the universe, where I am alone but not alone. Where I know I exist but do not exist. I would scream directly through their ears, but they couldn't hear me.

"Ned, it's time for dinner," Mom says softly.

He's twelve, his blond hair sticking up like he's just rolled out of bed. He walks down the stairs.

"I'm not hungry," he mutters, his voice barely audible as he tries to walk back to his room.

"You are eating whether you like it or not!" Mom yelled,

Ned slowly walked to the dining table and sat down.

Mom closes her eyes, taking a slow, shaky breath. Her eyes were shadowed with sleepless nights. She's trying to hold it together for Ned, for Dad. At least now she's trying but I see the cracks forming. Cracks that have always been there. It's just that nobody noticed. Late at night, when the house is still, I hear her muffled sobs. I sit beside her in the dark, unable to touch her, unable to take her pain away. I would sit next to her, as she watches our old family movies from our vacations.

Dad spends his days in the garage, pretending to fix something. Something that can't be fixed. The old car that's never going to run again. Mostly, he just sits there, staring at the tools. The house used to ring with his laughter—that deep, booming sound that could brighten even the gloomiest day. Now, it's just silence.

And me? I'm the ghost in my own house, trapped in this space I once called home. I've tried to leave. I walked to the front door and tried to step outside. But the air thickens, the world turns heavy, and I'm pushed back every time, as if the house itself won't let me go.

Even my room is barred to me. The doorknob refuses to turn beneath my hand, the door locked tight by some force I can't see. It's as if the house is keeping me out, hiding something within those four walls. I've pressed my ear against the door, hoping for a sound, a clue, but all I hear is an aching silence. It is the only place at the house where I couldn't get in. Mom, Dad or even Ned have not walked into my room. I need them to open the door.

#

"Ned please," Mom says, her voice breaking. A single tear slips down her cheek, and she wipes it away quickly, as if ashamed of it. Ned looks up at her, his blue eyes brimming with unshed tears, but he doesn't speak. He just stands, his chair scraping loudly against the floor, and runs upstairs. His door slams shut, and it was silence again.

Mom stays where she is, staring at the empty plate on the table. Her hands tremble as she picks it up and dumps the untouched food into the trash. She leans against the counter, her shoulders shaking as she buries her face in her hands.

I want to hold her, to tell her she's not alone. But I can't. I'm as helpless as they are.

The house feels different now as if it's grieving too. The house that used to be filled with laughter is now silent. The air inside is thick and heavy like the house is holding its breath, waiting for something. There's a wrongness here, a weight pressing down on me that has nothing to do with grief.

I close my eyes and search for the missing pieces of myself.

There has to be something.

Some fragment of memory that will explain why I'm still here. But every time I reach for it, it slips away, like sand sifting through my fingers.

This house is hiding something. I can feel it. And I have to find out what it is.

CHAPTER TWO—

NED

I watch Ned as he walks down the hallway, his small shoulders hunched, his steps hesitant like he's bracing for something he can't name. He would always glance over his shoulder, a quick flick of his head, and I felt his unease ripple through me. Does he sense me? I want to believe he does.

Ned has always been the most sensitive to the world around him, more so than anyone else in our family. When he was little, he would often point to a corner of his room and start laughing, his tiny arms reaching up toward the empty space. But there was never anyone there.

His big eyes always seemed to be searching for something no one else could see. I loved that about him. He was curious and full of wonder; the kind of kid who would notice the way sunlight danced on the floorboards or point out shapes in the clouds.

When he turned four, he started talking to someone.

It felt harmless—something Mom brushed off with a smile. "Oh, it's just a phase," she said when I brought it up. "Kids have imaginary friends all the time."

Maybe they did. I remembered having one too, but I outgrew it after a few weeks. Ned, though? He didn't let it go.

I'd catch him sitting in his room alone, murmuring softly under his breath. Sometimes he'd pause, like he was waiting for someone to answer. Then, out of nowhere, he'd laugh—his little giggle filling the room in a way that made my skin prickle.

"Who are you talking to?" I asked one afternoon, leaning against his doorway.

He turned to look at me, a smile tugging at his lips. "My friend."

"What friend?" I frowned, stepping inside. "There's no one here."

Ned tilted his head, his little brow furrowing like I was the one who didn't understand. He turned back to the empty space beside him, then patted the floor next to where he sat.

"Right here," he said simply.

I felt a shiver run down my spine. "Ned, there's no one there."

He looked up at me again, his smile faltering. "What do you mean there's no one there?"

The question made my stomach twist. I swallowed and forced a laugh. "No, I can't see anyone. There's no one there"

Ned shrugged like it didn't matter.

I tried to brush it off as nothing, but after that, I started paying closer attention.

It wasn't just the talking that got to me. It was the way he *played*.

Sometimes I'd hear him laughing in the backyard, running around with a wild, happy energy I hadn't seen in him before. I watched him from the window once—watched him pause mid-run, turn toward the empty air next to him, and giggle as though someone had whispered something funny. Then he'd nod and race off again, his arms flailing and his sneakers kicking up little puffs of dirt.

Other times, I'd find him sitting at the little table in his room, two teacups in front of him, one untouched. He'd chatter quietly, his little voice rising and falling as though carrying on a full conversation.

"Who are you talking to, Ned?" I asked once, leaning into the doorway.

He looked up at me, his small face bright with excitement. "We're doing storytelling"

I frowned. "What story, with who?"

"I don't know. It's about you, though," he said matter-of-factly as if that made perfect sense.

"Me?" My voice cracked slightly. "What do you mean?"

Ned just smiled and shook his head, like he was holding onto a secret he didn't want to share.

It was unsettling. Kids made up games, I knew that. But the way Ned talked, the way he *listened* to this invisible friend, felt different. Real.

One night, I woke up to the sound of voices coming from Ned's room. I rubbed my eyes and checked the clock—just after midnight. I groaned, pulling myself out of bed and shuffling toward his room.

"Ned?" I whispered, pushing the door open.

He was sitting on the edge of his bed, his legs swinging, and he was talking softly to the empty space in front of him.

"Don't worry," he murmured. "I'll keep it safe."

My heart skipped a beat. "Ned, what are you doing?"

He looked over his shoulder at me, blinking slowly, as though surprised to see me there. "Nothing. Just talking."

"To who?"

He looked back at the space in front of him, then at me. "My friend."

I hesitated. The air in the room felt colder than it should've. My eyes darted to the corner, half-expecting to see something—or someone—there. "What did your friend say to you?" I whispered.

Ned smiled faintly; his voice low. "My friend is going to watch me."

The hair on the back of my neck stood up. "Watch you?"

"Yeah." He tilted his head like it was no big deal. "

I forced a laugh, though my voice shook. "Well, you tell your friend it's bedtime, okay? No more talking tonight."

Ned grinned and nodded. "Okay."

I backed out of the room, my heart pounding in my chest. I couldn't explain it, but something about that night stuck with me. The way he looked past me when I spoke, the way he whispered like he *wasn't alone*—it didn't feel like pretend.

#

I miss those nights when we just lay on the trampoline in the backyard, pointing out constellations and making up stories to go with it. Ned would listen, wide-eyed, as I wove tales about the boy who left Earth, and lived alone somewhere in the universe far, far away. He'd ask if he could leave Earth too so he could reach the stars.

Now, the stars feel farther away than ever.

When Ned turned eleven, he started spending most of his time playing video games and hanging out with his friends. The time we spent together grew less and less with each passing day. I knew it was part of growing up, but that didn't make it hurt any less.

My little brother—the one with the chubby cheeks, who used to run to my room whenever he had nightmares, who followed me everywhere like a shadow and begged me to read him stories at night when Mom couldn't—was gone.

Now, there was an awkwardness in the way he looked at me, the stiffness in his body when I tried to hug him. He'd pull away too quickly, his face turning red, mumbling something about being "too old for that."

It was never the same after that.

\#

Ned pauses at the base of the stairs, his hand gripping the railing. I see him glance back again, his blue eyes darting to the shadows. A shiver runs through him, and he tightens his grip. "Ellie?" he whispers, so softly I almost miss it. My heart aches at the sound of my name on his lips.

I want to answer him, to tell him I'm here, but the words die in my throat. Instead, I follow him as he climbs the stairs, his steps slow and deliberate. The wood groans beneath his weight, the sound loud in the stillness of the house. He hesitates outside his bedroom door, his fingers brushing the doorknob before he pushes it open.

His room is almost exactly as I remember it. The astronaut poster I gave him still hangs on the wall, its edges curling slightly. I can see him the day I bought it, his face lighting up as I handed it to him. "For your first rocket ship," I'd teased, and he'd laughed, his cheeks turning red.

Ned sits on the edge of his bed, his head bowed. His small hands clutch at the edges of his sweater, and I can see the tears building in his eyes.

The chill in the room deepens, and I know he feels it. I want to wrap my arms around him, to tell him I miss him too, but all I can do is stand there, helpless. He shivers, pulling his knees up to his chest, and I see his gaze dart around the room like he's searching for me.

For a moment, I think I see recognition in his eyes, a flicker of something that tells me he knows I'm here. But it's gone just as quickly, leaving only the ache of unanswered questions.

"I'm here, Ned, I whisper, though I know he can't hear me. "I'll always be here."

I hover near the window in Ned's room, watching him scramble to get ready for school. His blonde hair is a mess, and he's muttering to himself as he shoves books and papers into his worn backpack. I've seen him do this a hundred times, but something is comforting in the way he's still just Ned—messy, rushed, always running late. He is mature for his age though. I would sometimes think he is older than me, but I am four years older.

"Where is it?" he mumbles, crouching down to check under his desk. A pen rolls off the edge, hitting the floor with a faint clatter. He sighs and gets down on his knees, leaning over to peek under the bed.

And then he freezes.

I feel it immediately—the sharp change in the air, the way his body goes rigid. His hand stops mid-reach, and his breath catches. Slowly, Ned leans back, his face turning pale as if all the blood has drained away. His blue eyes are wide, unblinking, locked on whatever he's just seen.

What is it? I move closer, my curiosity burning. I want to see what he's looking at, but I can't. From where I'm standing, all I can make out is the darkness under the bed and the faint glint of something metallic.

"Ned?" Mom calls from downstairs, her voice muffled but impatient. "You're going to miss the bus!"

He doesn't answer. He stays kneeling on the floor, staring into the shadows. His hand twitches, like he wants to reach out but is too afraid. I watch him closely, trying to piece it together. What could scare him like this?

Finally, he moves. Slowly, shakily, Ned sits back on his heels and closes his eyes. He takes a deep breath, then another, his small chest rising and falling like he's trying to calm himself. When he opens his eyes again, the fear is still there, but he's forcing himself to move. He grabs his backpack, slings it over one shoulder, and bolts for the door without a second glance.

As he runs down the stairs, I stay behind, staring at the spot where he had been frozen just moments before. What did he see? The question lodges itself in my mind, refusing to let go.

Something isn't right. Ned's never been afraid of the dark or the shadows under his bed.

But whatever he saw—whatever made him pale like that—it's something I can't ignore.

I move closer to the bed, leaning down as much as I can, though I already know I won't find anything. The space beneath it is empty, just like always. Still, the air feels heavier here, colder. My fingers itch with the need to touch, to pull back the layers of mystery that seem to thicken around me.

Whatever Ned saw, I must know. And for the first time since I've been trapped here, I feel a spark of something new—a need, sharp and urgent, to uncover what's hiding in the shadows of this house.

CHAPTER THREE

— MOM

I remember the way Mom's hands felt when I was little—soft but strong, always warm. She'd hold my hand tightly as we crossed the street, her thumb brushing over my knuckles as if she could protect me from the whole world. Some nights, when the rain was pounding against the windows, she'd sit with me on the couch, wrapping us both in her favorite quilt. We'd sip hot chocolate and watch the storm together. "You're safe, Ellie," she'd whisper, her voice soft but steady. And I believed her.

"Why don't you just say it?" Mom's voice is sharp, cutting through the heavy air of the house. "You think it's my fault, don't you?"

"I didn't say that," Dad snaps back, his tone low but no less biting. "But you've been acting like you know something. Something you're not telling me."

"You're ridiculous," she fires back. "You're the one who—""You're the one who—"

The words hang in the air, unfinished and heavy. I can't help but wonder what Mom meant by that. What could she be accusing Dad of? What secrets are they hiding from each other, from me? The phrase echoes in my mind, growing louder with every second of silence that follows.

"Don't," Dad interrupts, his voice suddenly cold. "Don't you dare."

There's a tense silence, broken only by the sound of Ned's school bus pulling away outside. I hover at the top of the stairs, torn between wanting to know what they're fighting about and hating the way their words cut through the walls. I've never heard them like this before, and it makes me feel even more invisible, like a ghost caught between worlds.

"You've been acting strange ever since—" Mom's voice falters, and I can almost hear the tears behind her words. "Ever since Ellie…"

"Don't you think I know that?" Dad shouts. His voice cracks and the sound of it makes something ache deep inside me. "Do you think this is easy for me? Losing her? Living in this house like nothing's changed?"

"Then why are you blaming me?" Mom's voice is quieter now, but the pain in it is sharper than any scream. "You don't think I've lost her too?"

There's a long silence, and then I hear the front door slam. Dad's car engine roars to life, and I watch from the window as he speeds off down the street. Mom is left standing in the kitchen, her shoulders slumped, her hands trembling as she grips the counter. For a moment, she looks like she might collapse.

She grabbed a bottle of pills in front of her. Her hair is disheveled, her face pale and drawn. She swallows two pills with a glass of water, her hand shaking as she sets the glass down.

#

The last time I saw Mom taking pills was after Ned was born. I remember the hushed conversations Dad would have with the doctor; the way he tried to shield me from what was happening. I was only four, but I remember the look in her eyes—lost, distant, like she wasn't really here anymore. Dad said she was just tired, but tired doesn't explain the nights she sat on the floor crying or the way she almost broke when Ned wouldn't stop crying for hours.

There was that day though, the day that's always been in my memory. It was mid-December, just before Christmas. The house smelled like cinnamon and pine, and soft holiday music played from the kitchen radio. Mom was bathing Ned in the small plastic tub by the bathroom sink. Her movements were slow, and mechanical like she was moving through a fog. Her eyes stared blankly at the water as if she wasn't even there.

I stood in the doorway, watching, uneasy but too young to understand the weight of what I was seeing. Something felt wrong. Ned started to slip, his small arms flailing as he splashed. The water rippled over the sides, but Mom didn't move. She just kept staring, her hands frozen.

"Mom!" I shouted, running in and grabbing her arm. The sound of my voice seemed to snap her out of it. She blinked, startled, and suddenly she was back, pulling Ned out of the water. He was coughing and crying, but he was okay. I wasn't sure she even realized what had happened.

After that, Mom was gone for a while. Dad said she went to visit Grandma, but I heard Dad talking on the phone one day.

"When can she be discharged? We need her home soon" Dad whispered on the phone.

He told me it was just to help her rest, but even as a kid, I knew it was more than that. The fear in his eyes told me everything I needed to know.

Now, watching her shake as she swallows the pills, I can't help but wonder: what if she's slipping again? And what if this time it's worse? What if— my breath catches—what if she did something to me? What if this house and all its darkness are because of her? The thought twists in my chest, sharp and wrong, but it's there, and I can't ignore it. Her hair is disheveled, her face pale and drawn. She doesn't notice me standing there, watching her. I wish I could tell her to stop, to hold her, and remind her of the strength she used to have. But I can't.

Instead, I just stand there, invisible, helpless, and aching with the weight of her grief. I don't know what's tearing her and Dad apart, but it feels bigger than just me. It feels like the house itself is feeding on their pain, pulling them further and further into the darkness. And I don't know how to stop it.

#

Mom had always been fragile in ways I didn't understand as a child. There were days when she wouldn't come out of her room, claiming she needed quiet to think. Other days, she'd be so energetic and happy, baking cookies or organizing closets as if nothing had ever been wrong. It was like living with two different versions of her. I never understood how Dad managed it.

There was a time when I was 10 and Ned was 6, it's a typical dinner at home. Ned and I were laughing about how Dad is munching his food so loud. My mom suddenly stood up, and threw away all the food, Just like that. She would snap.

Mom also likes being in control. That's probably why she loses her mind. She tries to control everything that's beyond her control. There was a time when I was at Anne's house for a sleepover with my other friends. At 11 p.m., she rang the doorbell. Anne's mom opened the door.

"I am taking my daughter home"

"Is everything okay?" Anne's mom muttered

Just like that. Mom came and took me home. "Why Mom? Why? I asked. We've talked about this, and you told me I could go?"

She was just quiet. No words were uttered on that drive back home. I felt embarrassed.

That's when I started losing friends. They would call my mom crazy and weird.

It felt like she wanted me to be a prisoner at our own house. At least now I am. I can't leave.

There was another time—more recent—that stays with me. She found a love letter in my backpack, something Ethan had written to me. I hadn't even noticed it was there. But when she saw it, something in her broke. Her face turned pale, then red, and then she started shouting, tearing through my things like she was searching for more. She demanded to know who Ethan was, what I had done, what secrets I was keeping from her. Her voice rose higher and higher until it wasn't even words anymore—just screams.

Dad had to step in, pulling her away as she collapsed on the floor, clutching the torn letter. I remember her sobbing, her hands trembling as she gripped the pieces of paper. "You're my little girl," she kept saying, over and over.

The other version of Mom is quite different. She would cook, she would clean, and she would open all the blinds so the natural light could beam inside our house, she would take me to the nail salon. She would take me to the shop with her. She would crack jokes, and Ned and I would start laughing so hard until it hurt. I could see the light in her eyes that I could barely see. I've always wished this version of her could last longer than the other version of her. But it doesn't last long.

And now she's broken. She's been broken…She's *always* been broken.

CHAPTER

FOUR— ETHAN

Ethan's name burns through my thoughts, demanding my attention. I remember his lopsided grin; the way he'd nervously brush his dark hair back when he saw me coming down the school hallway.

He wasn't supposed to exist in my world. Mom would've never approved. That's why it was all a secret—the notes we'd pass, the late-night texts, and the times he'd sneak over after everyone was asleep. My stomach twists as more memories push through the fog.

The love letter. Mom had found it in my backpack. It wasn't meant for her eyes, and the way her face darkened as she read it still chills me. She tore through my things, screaming about betrayal, about how I was too young for a boyfriend, about how I had kept this from her. She demanded I tell her everything about him, but I stayed silent. How could I explain Ethan to her? She wouldn't understand.

"Ethan…" I whisper, the name leaving my lips like a question. Where is he now? What happened to him?

And then something sharp pierces through my haze of thought—a memory, so clear it feels like it just happened. Ethan and I, together. His hand held mine tightly as he whispered, "No matter what happens, I won't let anything hurt you."

But the moment after that? It's gone.

I clutch onto the memory like it's a lifeline, my heart racing with the weight of the realization. I need to remember more. I need to know what happened to Ethan.

Where is Ethan?

Will I ever see him again?

I wasn't even able to attend my funeral. Just like in the movies, I should've been standing next to my coffin, hearing the final words my loved ones had to say. I should've watched them gather, listened to the memories they cherished, and seen the tears they cried for me. A part of me wanted to hear it— to know I mattered; to know I left a piece of myself in their hearts.

I needed to hear it. I needed to see them say goodbye. But I couldn't. I couldn't leave this place, no matter how hard I tried.

The thought gnaws at me, making this limbo feel even more unbearable. What did they say about me? Did Ned speak about all the times I helped him with his homework or shared my snacks with him when Mom wasn't looking? Did

Dad talk about the way I'd beg him to play his old guitar? Did Ethan… Did he even come? Did he cry? Or was he just… gone?

I imagine myself standing there, invisible, watching it all unfold. Mom clutching Ned close, both broken. Dad, is silent and stiff, unable to meet anyone's eyes. And Ethan—his head down, his hands trembling. I want it to be real, to see them all one more time, even if I can't touch them. But this house holds me captive.

This is the ghost I am—stuck in this place, bound by its walls, and haunted by what I can see or hear.

#

Ethan. His name lingers in my mind, warm and heavy. We weren't just in love; we were everything to each other. It wasn't the kind of fleeting romance that came and went in high school hallways. It was deeper, quieter, like a current beneath still water.

He made me feel seen like every glance he gave me was a promise.

I remember one crisp autumn afternoon, the leaves painting the ground in fiery hues. We were sitting by the old park bench near the school, where no one ever went. The air smelled of earth and something faintly sweet, like the scent of cinnamon wafting from a nearby bakery. I was rambling about how much I hated math class, and he was pretending to listen, though his eyes stayed locked on mine.

"Ellie," he said suddenly, his voice softer than the breeze.

"What?" I asked, laughing nervously.

"Do you know how beautiful you are?"

I froze, the words catching me off guard. My cheeks flushed, and I tried to brush it off. "Shut up, Ethan."

But he didn't laugh. He just leaned closer, his eyes searching mine for something unspoken. "I mean it. You're the most amazing person I've ever met."

And then it happened. He kissed me. His lips were warm and soft, tasting faintly of the caramel candy he'd been eating earlier. The world seemed to be still like it was holding its breath for us. At that moment, nothing else mattered—no school, no parents, no secrets. Just us.

When we pulled away, my heart was pounding so hard I thought he might hear it. I didn't know what to say, so I just smiled, and he smiled back, his hand slipping into mine.

Now, thinking about that moment, a hollow ache forms in my chest. I didn't know it then, but that kiss was the start of something fragile and fleeting. Where are you, Ethan Oliver? What do you think about me? Do you miss me? Or have you moved on?

A chill runs through me, and I clutch onto the memory like a lifeline, desperate to hold onto the warmth he gave me. For the first time since I became this... ghost, I feel truly alone.

#

Ethan wasn't just anyone—he was the high school heartthrob, the guy every girl talked about in hushed tones during lunch. He had it all: good looks, confidence, and a smile that could light up the coldest day. He played hockey, of course. That was part of his charm—always out on the rink, his dark hair damp with sweat, and his jersey slung casually over his shoulder after practice. He was the star of the team, the one every coach banked on, and every teacher gave a little more leeway to.

But Ethan wasn't just the golden boy everyone saw. He was more than that, at least to me.

He paid attention to me, Ellie—the quiet girl who sat at the back of class sketching in her notebook. He noticed the little things about me that no one else seemed to care about, like the way I always tucked my hair behind my ear when I was nervous or how I'd light up when someone mentioned my favorite books. He didn't care that I wasn't the most popular, the smartest, or the loudest. To him, I mattered. But did I?

He came from a different world—his parents were rich, the kind of rich that bought new cars on a whim and took family vacations to Europe. But none of that ever seemed to matter when we were together. He'd joke about it, calling himself "privileged" in the most self-aware way, and then shift the conversation back to me, always making sure I felt seen.

He wasn't just my boyfriend; he was my escape, my sanctuary. I remember the warmth of his hand in mine, the way his eyes lit up when he laughed, and the quiet promises he made when no one else was listening. He wasn't perfect, but he was perfect for me.

And now, all I have are these fragments of memories—moments stolen from a life I barely understand anymore. Where is he now? Does he think of me when he stares at the hockey rink or has my name faded into the background of his busy, beautiful life? What was our last conversation? I just can't remember.

The ache in my chest grows heavier as I cling to the image of him. If I could leave this house, I'd find him. I'd tell him everything—how much he meant to me, how much I still feel tethered to him even in death. But I can't. I am, bound to this place, while the world outside moves on without me.

Somewhere, I think, Ethan is still out there. Alive. And maybe—just maybe—he's haunted by me, too.

CHAPTER FIVE —

DAD

I hover near the garage, where Dad spends most of his time these days. The air smells like motor oil and rust, a stale reminder of the car he's been "fixing" for years. Except now, it's not about the car. It's about the silence. He sits on the old stool, staring at the engine like it holds answers he'll never find.

Dad. He was always the solid one, the anchor in a storm, the steady voice that could pull you back from the edge. But now, he looks more like a ghost than I do. His eyes, once filled with warmth and laughter, are sunken, shadowed by sleepless nights. His broad shoulders, the ones that used to carry me when I was little, now slump under a weight I can't see but can almost feel.

"You're supposed to be the strong one," I whisper, knowing he can't hear me. "You're supposed to hold it all together."

But even anchors break.

I remember when I was little, how he used to scoop me up after work, his hands still rough from a day of work. "Ellie-girl," he'd say, spinning me around until I laughed so hard my cheeks hurt. He'd sing off-key to whatever song was playing on the radio, and I'd sing along, our voices blending into a joyful mess. He was my hero then—the man who could fix anything, who made the world feel safe.

Now, he's a man unraveling, piece by piece.

I watch as he picks up a wrench, turns it in his hands, and then sets it down again. He hasn't touched the car in days. It's like he comes here to escape, to be alone with the grief he hides from Mom and Ned. He mutters something under his breath, too soft for me to catch, and then he sighs— a long, broken sound that seems to echo in the empty garage.

I think about the last time I saw him smile. It was months ago before everything fell apart. He was teasing Mom about her terrible cooking, and she swatted at him with a dishtowel, laughing. Ned was trying to hide his grin, and I was pretending to be annoyed by Dad's jokes. It was one of those moments you don't realize is precious until it's gone.

Does he think about that day? That day that I couldn't remember. Does he wonder if there was something he could have done differently? He was always the fixer, the one who solved problems, the one who made things better. But he couldn't fix this. He couldn't save me.

"Dad," I whisper, moving closer.

I wish I could touch him, wrap my arms around him, and tell him that he doesn't have to carry this alone. But all I can do is watch as he buries his face in his hands, his shoulders shaking with silent sobs.

I've never seen him cry before.

Something sharp and cold lodges itself in my chest, and for a moment, I can't breathe. I want to scream, to shake him, to let him know I'm here. That I'm not gone—not entirely. But the house holds me back, just like it always does, and I'm left with nothing but the weight of my own helplessness.

He stands suddenly, brushing his hands over his face like he can erase the tears. He grabs the wrench again, gripping it so tightly his knuckles turn white. For a second, I think he's going to throw it, to release some of the anger I know is boiling inside him. But he doesn't. He just sets it down carefully, his movements deliberate, as if he's afraid of breaking something else.

"Ellie," he says softly, his voice cracking. My heart stops. Does he know I'm here? Can he feel me?

But then he shakes his head, his eyes filling with a grief so deep it feels like it might drown him. "I'm sorry," he whispers. "I'm so sorry."

And then he walks out of the garage, leaving me alone with the shadows and the silence.

#

I know it wasn't just the grief of losing me—it was the weight of secrets. Secrets I discovered too late to confront him about.

It happened a week before I became…this. I was at the mall with my friends, laughing and sipping overpriced coffee, when I saw him. Dad. My dad. Sitting in the corner of a fancy restaurant with a woman who wasn't Mom. She was beautiful, with sleek dark hair and a smile that sparkled under the dim lights of the restaurant.

I froze. My friends didn't notice—I made sure of that. "I'll catch up with you guys," I said quickly, ducking behind a planter that barely hid me. I couldn't believe what I was seeing.

Dad leaned in close to her, his hand brushing hers. He was smiling—really smiling, the way he used to smile at Mom. My stomach twisted into knots as I tried to make sense of it. Maybe it was nothing. Maybe it was work. Maybe it wasn't what it looked like.

But then he reached across the table, gently tucking a strand of her hair behind her ear. And I knew. My dad—the man who could fix anything, who made me feel safe, who loved Mom—was cheating.

I didn't confront him. I couldn't. Instead, I went home that night, my head spinning, my heart heavy with betrayal. I tried to act normal, sitting across from him at dinner, pretending I didn't notice the faint smell of her perfume clinging to his shirt. I kept waiting for him to look guilty, to say something, to do something that would explain it away. But he didn't. He just smiled at me, the same warm smile he always gave, like nothing had changed. But he looked at me like he knew I knew something.

Everything had changed.

Now, as I watch him, I wonder if he's thinking about her. Does he miss her, too? Did she mean more to him than Mom, than Ned, than me? The thought makes me sick, but I can't stop it. He wipes his face with his hands, and for a moment, I almost feel sorry for him. Almost.

Because as much as I loved him, as much as I still love him, he wasn't perfect. He made mistakes—big ones. And yet, seeing him like this, drowning in guilt and grief, I can't bring myself to hate him. He's still my dad, even if he broke all the rules.

I wonder if he's as haunted as I am.

And for the first time, I realize that maybe I'm not the only ghost in this house.

CHAPTER SIX—
LITTLE GIRL

For the longest time, I thought I was alone in this house.

I had gotten used to the silence, the way it swallowed every sound and made everything feel heavier. My house, every corner of this place I used to know—had become unrecognizable. I wandered through the halls like a shadow, watching my family move on as though I had never existed. I told myself there was no one left to care, no one left to find me.

But I was wrong.

It started with a laugh. Soft, like wind brushing through leaves. It didn't belong to my family. It didn't belong to me.

I followed the sound, my steps hesitant and quiet. That was the first time I saw her late at night.

"What the—" I whispered under my breath.

The laugh came again—clearer this time. My heart, or whatever ghostly version of it I still had thudded in my chest. It wasn't coming from my family. I followed the sound down the hall, my bare feet moving quietly over the creaky floorboards, until I reached the attic door.

It was cracked open. I could see faint moonlight streaming through the gap, pale and cold.

I hesitated. The attic was a place I used to avoid, full of forgotten junk and strange noises at night. But something pulled at me—like the sound was meant for me alone.

There, in the center of the attic, sat a little girl.

She was small, maybe four or five, her knees tucked beneath her as she traced patterns in the dust with one tiny finger. Her curls fell over her face, soft and dark, glowing faintly in the silvery light.

"Hey," I said softly, half-expecting her to vanish. "Who… who are you?"

She looked up at me. Her eyes were wide, dark, and curious. She didn't seem scared—she didn't seem anything. Just calm. Like she knew me already.

"You can see me?" I asked, my voice thin.

She tilted her head slightly and nodded.

I blinked. *Is she like me? Is she a ghost?*

My mind reeled. I hadn't seen anyone—anyone like me—since I ended up here.

She stood up then, brushing the dust off her dress. Her little face stayed blank, unreadable, but she smiled faintly—just enough to make me pause.

Without a word, she turned and walked toward the attic stairs.

I hesitated for only a second before following her. What else could I do?

#

The little girl became a part of my world after that.

I'd find her sitting cross-legged in the living room, her tiny hands folding and unfolding in her lap. Sometimes, she perched on the windowsill, fogging up the glass with her breath, drawing shapes I couldn't quite make out. Other times, she'd disappear for hours, and I'd catch myself *looking* for her—like I actually missed her when she wasn't there.

The little girl and I created our little world inside the house.

We played games in the attic, where the dust sparkled in the sunlight like tiny stars. I taught her how to draw silly faces in the fog on the windows, and she giggled every time I exaggerated the expressions.

Sometimes, we'd sit together in the living room, staring out the window as the rain fell softly outside. I'd talk about random things—memories of school, of summers spent with Ned, of moments I hadn't thought about in years.

"You don't get bored listening to me, do you?" I asked one day, glancing at her.

She shook her head, her smile soft and reassuring.

"Well, that makes one of us," I muttered, but the warmth in her eyes made me feel like maybe I wasn't so bad at this whole "being dead" thing after all.

The little girl had a playful side.

I'd catch her darting behind curtains, peeking out just enough for me to see the glint of her eyes before disappearing again. She liked to hide in the shadows, giggling when I tried to find her.

"Okay, okay, you win," I'd say, throwing my hands up in mock defeat.

She'd step out then, her small hands clasped behind her back, her expression proud but shy.

One evening, she led me into the living room. The moonlight filtering through the windows cast long, eerie shadows on the walls. She twirled in the light, her small figure spinning gracefully, her laughter filling the empty space.

"You're kind of good at this whole ghost thing," I teased, leaning against the doorway.

She stopped spinning and looked at me, tilting her head as though to say, *You're not so bad at it either.*

She never spoke. Not once.

"Who are you?" I asked her one afternoon. "Did you live here? Before me?"

She didn't look up, but I thought I saw her smile again.

"Or are you just… passing through?" I pushed. The idea sounded ridiculous even as I said it. Where would a ghost even go?

Still, she said nothing. She just kept staring down like she was thinking about something far away.

It drove me crazy. Who was she? Why was she here?

I couldn't stop thinking about her.

She haunted me in a way that no one else had.

I started whispering theories to myself, as though saying them out loud would make sense of everything.

"Maybe she's a ghost from the past," I muttered one night, pacing my room as she sat silently on the floor. "Maybe she used to live here—maybe her family left her behind."

She watched me without a word, her eyes following my every move.

"Or maybe you're just... passing by," I continued, my voice shaking. "Maybe this house is just a stop for you, and you'll leave one day."

My voice cracked as I said it, and I didn't know why.

I crouched in front of her then, staring into her wide, unblinking eyes. "What are you waiting for?" I asked softly. "Why are you here?"

Despite my questions, I couldn't deny how much lighter the house felt with her around.

When I sat in the living room, staring out the window at nothing, she sat beside me, her small legs swinging. When I wandered the empty halls, she followed close behind, her presence a quiet reassurance I didn't know I needed.

She was a puzzle I couldn't solve, a ghost I couldn't let go of.

But in the quiet moments, when her laughter echoed through the house, and her small hand brushed against mine, I realized something.

For the first time, I didn't feel alone.

CHAPTER 7—
THE DAY I
BECAME A GHOST

I sit in front of the door to my bedroom—the door that refuses to open. No one has come to unlock it. Not Mom, not Dad, not Ned. It feels like they've forgotten it exists, just as much as they've forgotten me. But I can't forget. I can't stop thinking that maybe the answer is in there, hiding in the shadows behind that door.

How did I die?

The question loops endlessly in my mind, and I can't stop the possibilities from spilling out, each one more unbearable than the last. Did I get sick? Was it some disease, something that snuck up on me while I was sleeping? Or was it something worse? Was I hit by a car on my way home from school? Did I not even see it coming?

Then, another thought creeps in, one I've been trying to ignore. What if it wasn't an accident? What if Mom… slipped through the cracks? What if her sadness, her spiraling mind, pulled her too far, and I became the consequence of it? Or worse—what if it was Dad? He's been carrying secrets, and I know one of them. I know what I saw. What if he couldn't risk me telling Mom about the woman at the restaurant?

The thought makes me shudder. I shake my head, trying to clear the swirling storm of doubt and fear. None of it makes sense, but then again, nothing does. I clench my fists, trying to force back the frustration bubbling inside me.

The answer has to be in my room. It's the only thing that feels right—the only place that feels like it's holding the truth.

I close my eyes and think back to the day I became… this. The day everything changed.

#

It started like any other morning. I woke up in my bed, the sunlight streaming in through the cracks in the curtains. The air felt heavy but normal; just another day waiting to begin. I stretched, yawned, and stepped out of bed. I reached out for my phone I couldn't find it. But as soon as I crossed the threshold of my room, the door slammed shut behind me. It wasn't the wind; it wasn't an accident. It was something else— something I couldn't see but could feel like the air had thickened and turned against me.

Darkness gathered around me, a suffocating presence that sent shivers down my spine. I remember hearing the muffled wail of sirens outside. Police cars. An ambulance. My chest tightened as I rushed to the window, my breath fogging the glass as I tried to see what was happening.

That's when I saw him. Ned. He was standing in the front yard, his small frame looking so fragile against the chaos around him. He wasn't crying—he was just staring, his face pale and his eyes wide with something I couldn't understand. He looked at the window where I was standing. I waved at him, but he didn't wave back. Instead, he just stood there, frozen, like he was looking at something he couldn't believe.

I frowned, confused, and banged on the window. "Ned!" I called out, my voice strong. But he didn't respond.

Something was wrong.

I turned and ran down the stairs, my heart pounding in my chest. The front door was open, just a crack, and I rushed toward it, hoping to step outside, to see what was going on. But the moment I reached for the doorknob, it was like the house itself fought back. A force—heavy and invisible—wrapped around me, dragging me backward. No matter how hard I tried, I couldn't leave. I couldn't take a single step outside.

I crumpled to the floor, helpless, as the sound of footsteps and crying filled the house. My family came back inside, their faces drenched in tears, their voices shaking.

"I can't believe this is happening," Mom sobbed, her hands clutching at her chest.

Dad said nothing, his silence somehow louder than her cries. Ned ran back up to his room sobbing.

I tried to talk to them. I screamed their names, begged them to hear me, to see me, but they didn't.

It was like I didn't exist. The realization hit me like a cold wave, stealing the air from my lungs.

I was gone.

Now, as I sit in front of my bedroom door, I can't stop thinking about that day. The way Ned looked at me through the window—had he seen me? Had he seen me standing there, waving, trying to reach him? Or was he looking at something else entirely?

The frustration builds, sharp and hot, threatening to consume me. I slam my hands against the door, the sound echoing through the empty hallway. "Let me in!" I scream, my voice breaking. "Why won't you let me in?"

The house doesn't answer. It just sits there, silent and unyielding, keeping its secrets locked away.

But I won't stop. I can't stop. Somewhere in this house is the truth, and I'm going to find it—even if it tears me apart.

CHAPTER EIGHT

—THE

REFLECTION

Frustration builds up inside me like a storm, refusing to settle. I can't take this anymore. Days feel like months. I am losing it. I need answers. If my bedroom door won't open, then I'll find something somewhere else. There must be a clue in this house—anything to tell me what happened.

I search every corner. I tear through the silence, room by room. First, I go to Dad's garage. It smells of oil and dust, and the tools lie untouched, arranged neatly as if they've been waiting for him to come back to life. But there's nothing here—no sign of what I'm looking for.

Next, I go to Mom's closet. Her clothes hang limply, untouched for days, maybe weeks. The faint scent of lavender clings to them, but they feel as lifeless as I do. I dig through the drawers, desperate for something, anything, that might explain what happened to me. But there's nothing.

The house feels like it's mocking me, its silence pressing in closer as I search every empty space. Finally, I find myself back in Ned's room, where he froze that day, staring under the bed. My chest tightens as I crouch down, leaning in to see what he saw.

At first, it's just shadows and dust. Then, tucked in the farthest corner, I see it: an old mirror, cracked and tilted at an odd angle. It's the one Mom broke months ago when she was having one of her episodes and never bothered to throw away.

The jagged edges catch the faint light, distorting the reflection. I reach out, brushing my fingers near it, and the air grows colder.

That's when I see it—the reflection of the bedroom door behind me.

Ned must've seen something that day. He must've seen me, standing there in the reflection. My heart races as the realization sets in. He saw me. He *saw* me.

Maybe that's why he froze. Maybe that's why he looked so pale, so terrified.

I pull back from the mirror, my mind spinning. If Ned saw me then, maybe—just maybe—I can use this. Maybe I can reach him. Maybe I can make him understand. If I can get him to see me again, perhaps he can open the door to my room. Maybe he can set me free.

#

The dining table felt colder than usual, the silence heavy and suffocating. Dinner was set—a steaming bowl of pasta, a loaf of bread on a chipped ceramic plate, and a small salad no one seemed interested in. Mom had cooked the pasta, though her movements in the kitchen were as robotic as ever. She didn't even scold Ned for eating too fast or for not thanking her.

Ned finished his meal in record time, pushing his chair back without a word. His small frame looked even smaller under the weight of whatever he was feeling. He didn't look at Mom or Dad as he slipped out of the dining room, heading straight to his bedroom. I followed him, my curiosity and frustration building with each step.

Inside Ned's room, I stood in the corner, watching him flopped onto his bed. He didn't turn on the light, letting the dim glow of the hallway seep in through the cracked door. I wanted so badly to reach him, to shake him, to make him understand that I was still here.

"Ned!" I screamed, the sound raw and desperate. But he didn't flinch. He couldn't hear me. I screamed again, louder this time, but it was like yelling into a void. Hopelessness clawed at me as I scanned his room, searching for anything I could move, anything that might make him feel my presence. I focused on his water bottle, his favorite action figure, and even his crumpled hoodie on the chair. But no matter how hard I tried, my hands passed through them like smoke.

Frustrated, I left his room, the familiar ache of failure pressing down on me. I found myself back in front of my bedroom door. The door that refused to open. The door that felt like it held all the answers I couldn't reach.

"Open the door!" I screamed, slamming my hands against the wood. The sound echoed through the hallway, sharp and hollow. "Please, open up! Why won't you let me in?"

I banged harder, my cries turning into sobs. "Please!" I whispered, my forehead resting against the door. "I need to know. I need to remember."

I banged so hard I couldn't stop.

And then I heard it. The creak of Ned's door opened behind me.

I turned, tears still streaming down my face. Ned was standing there, his small frame silhouetted in the dim light. He looked so fragile, so hesitant as if he wasn't sure what he was doing. His eyes darted toward me—no, toward the door I was standing in front of.

He heard me. He *heard* the banging.

I froze, watching as he stepped closer. Each movement was slow, deliberate, his bare feet making the faintest sound on the floor. He stopped just in front of the door, his hand hovering over the doorknob.

For a moment, he just stood there, staring at the door as if he could feel the weight of everything behind it. And then, slowly, he turned the knob and pushed it open.

CHAPTER NINE
—THE BEDROOM

The door creaked open slowly as Ned stepped inside, his small frame illuminated by the dim light of the hallway. He moved like a ghost himself, silent and deliberate, his head down as he shuffled toward my bed. I watched him, stunned, unsure if he could see me or feel my presence. He didn't say anything. He just curled up on my bed, pulling the blanket over his trembling shoulders.

I stood frozen in the doorway, unable to comprehend what was happening. For the first time since I became this... thing, the door to my bedroom was open. The invisible barrier that had kept me out was gone. Tentatively, I stepped inside.

Everything looked exactly as I had left it. My walls were still covered in posters of my favorite bands and quotes scribbled in marker. My desk was cluttered with notebooks and pens, my favorite sketchbook lying open to a half-finished drawing of a tree. The faint scent of vanilla lingered in the air from the candle I always burned when I studied. Even the small string of fairy lights around my window was still in place, though they were dark now.

I turned my gaze to the music player on the nightstand. It was an old, battered thing, but it still worked. As I approached, the player flickered to life on its own, filling the room with the soft melody of *"Gravity"* by Sara Bareilles.. My favorite song. My throat tightened as the music swelled, a haunting reminder of who I used to be.

I stood there for a moment, letting the music wash over me before my eyes were drawn to my desk. A piece of paper sat in the middle, slightly askew as if it had been hurriedly placed there. My stomach twisted as I moved closer, the song playing in the background like a cruel soundtrack to the moment. My hands trembled as I picked up the paper, the words scrawled across it in my own handwriting, sending a chill down my spine.

I'm sorry.

That was the first line. My eyes scanned the rest of the note, the words blurring as I read them.

I can't do this anymore. I'm tired. I feel like I'm drowning, and no one can save me. Mom, Dad, Ned—I love you so much, but I can't keep pretending I'm okay. I'm not okay. Please forgive me.

A wave of shock and horror crashed over me as the note fell from my hands, drifting to the floor. It couldn't be true. It couldn't. But the evidence was staring me in the face, written in my own words.

I had done this.

I had ended my own life.

It wasn't Mom or Dad or anyone else. It wasn't some accident or some illness. It wasn't the house. It was me. I was the reason for their grief, for their brokenness. I had shattered my family, and now I was trapped here, a ghost of my own making.

My knees buckled, and I sank to the floor, the song still playing softly in the background. The little girl was just watching me, keeping me company, but her presence gave me a sense of comfort, that I was not alone. My hands covered my face as sobs wracked my body. How could I have forgotten? How could I have done this to myself, to them?

Through my tears, I glanced at Ned, who was still curled up on my bed.

"Ned," I whispered, my voice cracking. "I'm so sorry. I'm so sorry."

He stirred slightly, his breath catching as if he heard something. I froze, staring at him as his eyes fluttered open. He sat up slowly, looking around the room, his gaze lingering on the music player, then the desk. For a moment, I thought he might see me, that he might know I was there. But he just sat there, silent and still, the weight of the room pressing down on both of us.

And then, as quietly as he had entered, he slipped off the bed and walked back toward the door. He paused, his hand resting on the doorknob, before glancing back at the room one last time.

"Ellie, I heard you knocked that night, but I didn't let you in, I'm sorry" he whispered, so softly

I almost didn't hear it. Then he left, closing the door behind him.

The room was silent now, the song fading into nothing. And I was alone again, alone with another ghost, the little girl just staring at me as I stared at the note that had shattered everything. I remember now. All the memories that were lost. All the pain I felt that day. I was broken.

I remember everything.

CHAPTER TEN— THE DAY I FELL APART

I remember now, the exact moment everything shattered.

The day had been heavy, the kind of gray afternoon where the air felt too thick to breathe. I'd been walking across the school courtyard, my mind buzzing with what I needed to tell Ethan. My hands were shoved into my hoodie pocket.

I was nervous but hopeful. I had to talk to him.

But then I saw him.

The library windows stretched along the back of the school, and just beyond them, near the far corner, I froze. Ethan was there. And he wasn't alone.

A girl—tall, with her perfect ponytail and too-sweet smile—stood close to him, way too close. I felt my chest tighten as I watched her lean in, her hand resting lightly on his arm, her face tipping up toward his.

And then she kissed him.

It wasn't just a peck. It wasn't innocent. She lingered, and so did he.

I don't know if it was my gasp that did it or the way I stumbled forward like I'd been punched in the stomach, but Ethan looked up and saw me. His eyes widened, and for a second, we just stared at each other through the window, frozen.

Then he pushed her away.

"Ellie—wait!" I heard his voice before I even realized I was moving. My feet carried me around the library, toward the side door, as he jogged out to meet me. The girl had already disappeared into the building, leaving us alone under the gray sky.

"What was that?" I demanded, my voice sharper than I intended. I stopped walking, planting myself on the pavement as Ethan skidded to a halt a few feet away.

"It's not what you think," he said quickly, his hands going up defensively. "She kissed me, Ellie! I didn't—"

"You didn't stop her!" I cut him off, the words cracking in my throat. "I saw you. I *saw* you standing there, letting her do it."

I have heard it before. My best friend told me that she saw Ethan with another girl, holding each other's hand at the mall. But I refused to believe her. I lost my best friend because I thought she was just jealous that I was happy. But here we are, I saw it with my two eyes.

He ran a hand through his hair, his face flushed. "It wasn't like that. You don't understand—"

"What's there to understand, Ethan?" My voice shook as I forced the words out. "I came here to talk to you, and I found you *with her*. Who even *is* she?"

"It doesn't matter," he muttered, looking away.

"It matters to me!" I shouted, my voice breaking. My chest ached, and I wanted to scream at him, shove him, anything to make him hurt as much as I did in that moment. "You said you loved me, Ethan. Was that a lie? Were you just saying what I wanted to hear?"

He looked back at me then, his eyes dark with something I couldn't name—regret, guilt, or maybe just annoyance. "I don't have to explain myself to you, Ellie."

I froze, the air rushing out of my lungs. "What?"

"You're always like this," he said, his voice rising. "Always so… paranoid. Like I can't talk to anyone without you freaking out. It's exhausting!"

My hands trembled as I stared at him, my heart pounding so hard I thought it might break. "So it's *my* fault now?" I whispered. "You're blaming me?"

He didn't answer. He just looked at me, his face hardening as the silence stretched between us.

I swallowed back the tears threatening to spill. "You're walking away, aren't you?" I asked quietly.

Ethan's jaw clenched, but he didn't say anything. He just took a step back, his eyes flickering over me like he couldn't even stand to look at me anymore.

"You are exhausting, Ellie, you are just as crazy as your mom" were the last words he said."

I felt the world tilt under me as he turned and walked away, his feet fading against the pavement. I stood there, frozen, watching him disappear around the corner of the building.

I need to talk to you. The words that I never got to say.

It was just me. Alone.

#

When I got home that day, the weight of Ethan's words crushed me. I wanted to cry, to scream, to do something, but I couldn't. I was too numb, too lost.

I found Mom on the couch, staring blankly at the television. She didn't even look at me when I walked in. She's having one of her episodes again.

"Mom," I said softly, trying to keep my voice steady. "Can we talk? Please?"

"Not now, Ellie," she mumbled, her eyes fixed on the screen.

"Mom, please," I begged, my voice breaking. "I need you."

She turned her head slightly, her gaze empty and distant. "I said not now."

Her words hit me harder than Ethan's. I turned away, tears blurring my vision, and climbed the stairs. As I passed the landing, I glanced out the window and saw Dad in the garage. His phone was pressed to his ear, he was whispering, his free hand gesturing sharply.

For a moment, I thought about going to him. But then I remembered the woman I'd seen him with at the restaurant, the way he'd smiled at her, touched her hand. I felt sick.

Instead, I walked to Ned's door and knocked softly. "Ned?" I whispered, my voice trembling. "Can I come in?"

There was no response.

I could hear his video game. Too loud I couldn't even hear my voice.

I pressed my forehead against the door, fighting back tears.

Finally, I turned and walked to my room, closing the door behind me.

The weight of the day pressed down on me like an anchor. My room should've been a place of comfort, but instead, it felt like I was stepping into a space I no longer recognized. Everything looked the same—my bed neatly made, my desk cluttered with notes and doodles, the fairy lights framing the window—but I wasn't the same. I wasn't Ellie anymore. I was just a hollow version of the girl who used to belong here.

I sat on the edge of my bed, my hands gripping the edge of the blanket, and tried to breathe, but the walls felt like they were closing in. The fight with Ethan replayed in my head, his words echoing like a cruel melody.

"You're exhausting, Ellie." "You're just as crazy as your mom"."

Each one a dagger that sank deeper into my chest.

I thought I loved him. I thought he loved me. But he didn't. I was just another girl to him, a fleeting thing he could use and throw away when it got too complicated. The boy I had trusted with my heart had ripped it to pieces, and now I was left holding the shards.

And Mom—how could she not see me? How could she not care? I tried to tell her, I tried so hard, but she was too far gone. She couldn't be the mother I needed. Maybe she never could. And Dad—he was a stranger now, caught up in his secrets, his lies. The man I once believed could fix anything had destroyed everything. And Ned, he's no longer the Ned I used to know.

I felt the tears coming, hot and relentless, spilling down my cheeks as I buried my face in my hands.

The loneliness was unbearable, a suffocating force that left me gasping for air.

I wanted to scream, to rip the walls down, to make someone—anyone—see me, hear me, save me. But there was no one.

I glanced at my desk, at the picture frame sitting near the edge. It was a photo of me, Ned, Mom, and Dad taken years ago at the park. I was holding Ned's hand, grinning at the camera while Dad had his arm around both of us. We looked happy. We looked whole. But it was a lie. It had always been a lie.

My gaze drifted to the mirror on my dresser, and for a moment, I didn't recognize the girl staring back at me. Her eyes were red and swollen, her face pale and tired. She looked broken. She looked like someone who didn't belong.

I leaned forward, my fingers brushing the surface of the mirror. "What happened to you?" I whispered, my voice cracking. But the girl in the mirror didn't answer. She just stared back at me, silent and empty.

For the first time in my life, I felt truly invisible. I wasn't Ellie anymore. I wasn't anything. I was a ghost, even when I was still alive.

I threw my phone in the mirror and picked up the shattered glass.

I remember the pain; I don't remember how long it lasted.

I remember feeling the blood gushing from my wrist. *I did not try to stop it*

.

Then, the memories from when I was little played out like a film, just like in the movies.

It was everything. It flashed before my eyes, pulling me back into the life I had almost forgotten.

Then, it was silent.

CHAPTER ELEVEN —THE DAY THE DOORBELL RANG

I was filled with emotions—rage, sorrow, and something else I couldn't name—as I drifted aimlessly through the halls of the house. My anger sat heavy in my chest like a storm waiting to break.

The little girl sat quietly on my bed, her tiny legs dangling over the edge. She stared at me with wide, knowing eyes, her face calm but unreadable. She never spoke, but she was always there, like a shadow keeping me company. I wanted to say something to her, ask her why she stayed, but the words never came.

I turned away, wandering again. My feet carried me up the stairs without direction, my mind a whirlwind of thoughts and regrets.

And then I heard it.

Ding-dong.

The sound of the doorbell rang through the house like a gunshot, sharp and sudden. I froze mid-step, my chest tightening.

I heard Mom's footsteps moving toward the door, slow and deliberate. The familiar creak of the hinges made the walls feel smaller, like they were closing in on me.

"Hi, Mrs. Miller," a voice said.

I knew that voice. *Ethan.*

It felt familiar and unfamiliar all at once, like a memory I wanted to bury. My fists clenched at my sides as I followed the sound, my anger bubbling just below the surface.

From the hallway, I saw Ethan standing in the doorway, clutching something in his hands—something small, wrapped in an old piece of cloth. He looked nervous, like he didn't want to be there, like the air in the house was too heavy to breathe.

"What do you want?" Mom's voice was cold, sharp. She folded her arms, her face unreadable.

Ethan swallowed, shifting his weight. "I, uh… I came to give you this." He held out the small bundle. "It's Ellie's. Someone from school cleaned out her locker and gave this to me. I thought… I thought you should have it."

Mom hesitated before reaching for it, unwrapping the cloth to reveal what was inside—my favorite notebook, a few photos, a pen she'd always carried with her. She stared at the items for a moment, her expression softening before it turned to something darker.

"Why are you really here, Ethan?" she asked quietly, her voice brittle.

Ethan's face fell. "Mrs. Miller… I need to tell you something."

Mom's eyes narrowed. "What is it?"

He hesitated, looking down at his hands before finally saying it. *"Ellie was pregnant."*

The words hung in the air like smoke, suffocating.

Mom froze, her face going pale as the realization hit her. "What did you just say?"

Ethan's voice broke. "She was pregnant."

Something inside me snapped.

It was a few days before we broke up, I took the test.

I had been feeling off for weeks—nauseous, exhausted, like my body was trying to tell me something I wasn't ready to hear. I remember buying the test at the drugstore, my hands shaking as I handed the cashier a crumpled bill, avoiding eye contact. I stuffed the box into my bag like it was a dirty secret and rushed home, my heartbeat loud in my ears.

I sat on the cold bathroom floor, staring at the test on the sink. It felt like time stopped while I waited. The silence was unbearable, and when I finally looked, there they were—two faint pink lines. Two lines.

The truth hit me like a wave, pulling me under, but I knew I had to tell Ethan. I *wanted* to tell him.

But then we fought. And then he walked away.

I stood there, tears streaming down my face, holding onto the words I couldn't say. *I'm pregnant. You're going to be a dad.*

But I never got the chance to tell him. I just watched him leave, not knowing he had already taken more from me than I could bear to lose. But how did he know? I never told him.

\#

I screamed. I screamed so loud and so violently that the walls seemed to shake. I stormed into the room, standing just inches from him, my rage pouring out in waves he couldn't feel or hear.

"You knew?" I screamed though he didn't look up. "You knew, and you still walked away." You let this happen!"

"She really didn't tell me Mrs. Miller, but I saw a pregnancy test in her purse; it had two lines in it; I didn't tell her that I knew; I was scared too"

The lights flickered wildly, the bulbs buzzing and popping in their sockets. Mom gasped, looking up at the ceiling.

And then it happened.

CRASH!

"What was that?" My mom uttered.

The vase on the hallway table shattered, and pieces of porcelain flew across the floor.

The little girl appeared suddenly, standing in the corner with her hands pressed tightly over her ears. Her eyes were wide, filled with fear, and for the first time, she looked as small and fragile as I felt.

"No," I whispered, my anger shifting into something else. "No, I didn't mean to—"

She disappeared.

My breath caught in my throat, but no one noticed.

I stood beside Mom, watching Ethan's retreating back as he stepped outside. He paused at the threshold, his hand on the doorknob, but he didn't turn around.

"Ethan," I said softly, stepping closer. "I have loved you with all my heart." My voice wavered as I fought the tears building in my eyes. "But you weren't real to me. I thought it was real—*we* were real. How could you?"

I turned to look at Mom, who stood in the doorway, her arms still crossed tightly over her chest. Her lips parted, and for a moment, I thought she might have *heard* me. Not my words, but my pain.

Mom turned back to Ethan, her face a mask of fury. "You should be ashamed, you know?" she said, trembling. "I never liked you. It's not like there was anything *to like.* But I knew my daughter loved you. For her to lie to us, to sneak around behind our backs, to hide this…" She shook her head, tears shining in her eyes. "I heard the late-night phone calls. I saw the way she smiled when you messaged her. You took the light out of her eyes, Ethan. You should be *sorry* for that."

Ethan looked broken, his shoulders slumping as though the weight of her words crushed him. He opened his mouth to say something but stopped himself, turning toward the door.

She wiped her eyes quickly and muttered, "You should go now."

Ethan nodded and slipped out the door, leaving us in silence.

I stared at Mom as she stood there, her face softening as she gazed into the empty hallway. For a moment, it felt like she had said everything I wanted to say—like her words carried the weight of my own, the things I couldn't say myself.

I couldn't believe it.

My mom—*my mom*, who I thought never paid attention, who always seemed so far away—had spoken up for me. She had seen me, even when I thought I was invisible.

The anger that had burned so fiercely in my chest seemed to lift, little by little, like smoke dispersing into the air. I felt lighter, the weight I'd been carrying for so long easing just a bit.

CHAPTER TWELVE— MOVING ON

I've been watching them for weeks now. My family is trying—trying to breathe again, to live again—but it's messy, fragile, like a house of cards built on shaking ground. Yet, even in the chaos, there's something new. It's small, almost imperceptible at first, but it's there—a flicker of hope.

Ned is the first to start piecing things together. I can see it in the way he's been spending more time at the dinner table, even when the silences stretch too long. He's started talking about me—not in a sad way, but in a way that keeps me alive. He told Mom and Dad about the time we stayed up late in the backyard, watching for shooting stars. He told them how I helped him learn the constellations, how I made up ridiculous names for the ones we couldn't find.

"I think Ellie called it 'The Rocket Ship That Got Lost,'" he said, his voice shaky but steady. I watched from the corner of the room as Mom and Dad exchanged glances, their faces softening. It wasn't much, but it was enough to spark something in them. A shared memory. A shared loss. For a moment, they weren't alone in their grief.

Mom has been trying too. She's cooking again, though her movements are slower, more deliberate, as if every step takes effort. But she's present. She hums quietly to herself as she moves around the kitchen, her voice barely audible but there. I cling to those moments, to the small signs of her coming back to us—or rather, to Ned and Dad. I know she can't see me. She probably never could. But I hope she feels me, somehow.

And Dad… Dad is the hardest to watch. He's still carrying so much guilt. He stays up late in the living room, staring at old photo albums. Sometimes, I catch him flipping through pictures of me as a kid—birthday parties, family trips, the moments when we were happy, or at least looked like we were. I want to tell him it's okay. I want to tell him I understand.

And that I have forgiven him.

But all I can do is sit beside him in the silence.

#

One evening, Ned went into my room. He walked in, almost hesitant, and sat on my bed. He didn't say anything, just looked around the room like he was trying to memorize it. His fingers brushed over the music player on my nightstand, the one I used to use every night before bed. He pressed play, and my favorite song filled the air.

Hearing it again felt like someone had reached inside me and found the part of me that still hurt the most. I watched Ned close his eyes, letting the music wash over him. Maybe he played it for me. Maybe he played it for himself. Either way, it felt like a connection—a thread tying us together, even if he didn't know it.

He stayed there for hours that night, flipping through my books and drawing on scraps of paper from my desk. At one point, he found my journal. I froze, unsure of what he would think, unsure of what he would find. But he didn't open it right away. He just held it, his hands trembling slightly as if he knew it was something sacred.

The house doesn't feel as heavy anymore. The air is still thick with memories, but there's a lightness creeping in—a warmth that wasn't there before. The trampoline in the backyard creaks again as Ned jumps on it with his friends. Mom hums as she cooks, her hands steady, her movements sure. Dad plants flowers in the garden, bright splashes of color against the gray backdrop of the past months.

And me? I feel lighter too. I don't know if I'm ready to leave, but I know I'm closer. Watching them heal, even in their imperfect, stumbling way, gives me hope. They don't need me to fix them. They're learning to fix themselves.

One night, I sat in the corner of Ned's room as he opened my journal for the first time. He read quietly, his lips moving silently over the words. I could feel his emotions shifting with every page—sadness, laughter, love. When he reached the last entry, the last words I wrote on my journal, he paused, his breath catching.

"I didn't think anyone would notice I was gone," I had written. "I didn't think I mattered. But

I hope, someday, they'll remember the good things. I hope they'll remember I loved them."

Ned closed the journal, tears streaming down his cheeks. "I remember, Ellie," he whispered, clutching the book to his chest. "I remember."

Something inside me eased. The knot of pain and guilt and anger I had been carrying began to unravel. Ned remembered. And maybe Mom and Dad would too.

Healing isn't a straight path. It's a messy, tangled thing, full of setbacks and small victories. But it's happening. My family is breathing again, living again. And maybe—just maybe—it's time for me to let go. But how? What's holding me back still?

CHAPTER THIRTEEN-THE GOODBYE

Ned's voice fills the room, soft but trembling. He clutches my journal, reading aloud the words I once poured out in desperation. "

I stand in the corner, my chest tightening with every word. He pauses, his lips trembling as he reads the last line again silently. The room feels heavier with his grief, and I want to run to him, to tell him I'm here. I want to hold him the way I used to when he had a bad dream or when he'd come home from school crying because the other kids teased him. But I can't. All I can do is stand there, helpless, watching his small shoulders shake as he cries.

"I miss you, Ellie," Ned whispers, hugging the journal tightly to his chest. His voice cracks, and I feel like my heart is breaking all over again. "I miss you so much."

"I miss you too," I whisper, knowing he can't hear me. "I never left."

And then, I feel it. The pull. It starts as a warmth in the pit of my stomach, spreading outward, wrapping around me like a comforting hug. The air grows lighter, the room brighter, and I know something is changing. Something is ending.

I glance at Ned, panic gripping me. I'm not ready to leave. He's still here, still hurting, still holding onto me like I'm the only thing keeping him afloat. How can I go now?

But the light grows stronger, and the pull becomes impossible to resist. It's gentle but firm like it knows what's best for me, even if I don't.

Memories flood my mind, rushing over me in a cascade of emotions. The first is small but warm—a cold winter morning when Ned was just a baby. Mom let me hold him on the couch, wrapping us both in a thick quilt. "Be careful with his head," she said, but her voice was soft, trusting. Ned smiled up at me, his tiny hand reaching out to grab my finger. "You're his big sister now," Mom whispered. "You'll always be there for him."

Then another memory—a summer afternoon in the backyard. Ned and I were running through the sprinklers, our laughter echoing against the house. The sun was hot on our skin, and the grass smelled fresh and earthy. Dad was grilling burgers on the patio, his deep voice singing along to an old rock song on the radio. Mom sat nearby, her hair pulled into a messy bun, sipping lemonade and smiling like everything in the world was perfect.

The memories come faster now, blending together in a blur of colors, sounds, and feelings. I remember Dad teaching me to ride my bike in the cul-de-sac, running alongside me as I wobbled and shrieked with laughter. I remember baking cookies with Mom, her hands guiding mine as we rolled the dough and sprinkled chocolate chips. I remember Ned sneaking into my room late at night because he had a nightmare, curling up next to me as I told him stories until he fell asleep.

But then the darker memories seep in, heavy and cold. I remember the fights between Mom and Dad, the way their voices rose like thunder, shaking the walls of our home. I remember the days Mom didn't get out of bed, and the emptiness in her eyes when she finally did. I remember finding Dad in the garage, his phone pressed to his ear, talking to someone who wasn't Mom.

And then, the memory I've tried so hard to bury—the day Ethan broke my heart. His cruel words, the way he walked away like I didn't matter. The way everything felt like it was falling apart all at once.

The memories swirl around me, each one a piece of the puzzle that led me here. The laughter, the love, the pain—it's all part of my story. It's all part of me.

He looks around the room, his eyes wide, and whispers, "Goodbye Ellie". He knew.

I step closer, the pull of the light growing stronger.

And there I saw the little girl, waiting for me. The little girl that kept me company. The little girl who watched quietly. Maybe it's time for her to go too?

The light was warm and inviting, pulling me toward it like it always had. This time, though, I wasn't afraid. The little girl stood beside me, her small hand tucked into mine, her face calm and peaceful.

I looked down at her, my heart—or whatever was left of it—filling with emotions I couldn't name.

"Is it time for you to go?" I whispered, my voice trembling.

I knelt to her level, brushing my fingers near hers, though we both were just fragments of something lost. "You never told me your name," I said gently.

For the first time, she spoke. Her tiny voice was soft and clear, like the faintest whisper of wind through the trees.

"I don't have one," she said, looking straight into my eyes. "Because you never named me."

The words hit me like a punch to the chest. My breath caught, and the tears I'd been holding back spilled over.

You never named me.

I fell back onto my knees, the weight of her words sinking in, spreading through me like ice. She was mine. The child I never gave a chance, the little life I carried and let slip away.

She smiled softly, that same knowing smile she'd given me the first time I saw her in the attic.

"I'm so sorry," I whispered, my voice breaking. "I didn't… I didn't know."

The little girl reached out and touched my hand, her fingers light and warm.

And then the memories came flooding back— Ned at four years old, sitting on his bedroom floor, talking to someone I couldn't see. "My friend," he'd called her. The laughter, the whispers, the way he'd look into the empty space beside him like someone was there.

The little girl.

She wasn't just a ghost of my regret—she had been *real* to Ned, all those years ago. She had been his "imaginary friend," the one he played with and trusted, long before I ever knew her. She had been part of our lives all along, long before I decided to be gone.

"You were with him," I whispered, my voice cracking as I stared at her. "You were there for Ned."

She nodded slowly, her soft curls bouncing as she looked at me with eyes far older than her tiny frame.

I covered my mouth, trying to hold back the sobs building in my chest. "How? How did you find him?"

She didn't answer, but she didn't need to. Somehow, in ways I couldn't begin to understand,

She had crossed and traveled in time and space to be part of our lives—reaching out to the only person who might have seen her.

She had been there all along, watching, waiting, trying to be seen before I even knew. The little girl who didn't get the chance to see the real world. It's all my fault. I trapped her in this house long before I decided to just be gone.

"Forgive me" That's all there is to say.

My body feels weightless, my mind clear. The pain, the guilt, the anger—it all melts away, replaced by a peace I've never known. I can hear my favorite song playing on a loop. I glance back one last time, taking in the sight of my little brother sitting on my bed, my journal clutched to his chest.

As I step fully into the light with my little girl, I feel everything I was, everything I am, expanding, becoming part of something bigger. And in that moment, I realize the truth.

This is the ghost I am—not the kind that haunts, but the kind that loves, the kind that lets go.
And then, I was gone.

I named her Hope.

THE END

If you are experiencing any mental health crisis, please reach out to someone or contact the Mental Health crisis hotline in your state.

www.ingramcontent.com/pod-product-compliance
Lightning Source LLC
Chambersburg PA
CBHW020045310726
48970CB00007B/2427